Harris the Hed
And His Running Adv.....

First published in 2018

Copyright © AV Turner 2018

The rights of the author and illustrator have been asserted in accordance with Sections 77 and 78 of the Copyright Designs and Patents Act, 1988.

All rights reserved.

ISBN-13: 978-1720617877

Follow: @AVTurnerAuthor

TEAMAUTHOR UK
Publishing with you

To my late mother, Janet

And all young runners...everywhere.

In loving memory of

Alastair Shakeshaft

1965–2018

Table of Contents

Chapter 1....................7

Chapter 2....................11

Chapter 3....................16

Chapter 4....................21

Chapter 5....................29

Chapter 6....................36

Chapter 7....................43

Chapter 8....................48

Chapter 9....................51

Chapter 10.................60

Chapter One

It was a warm sunny morning in September. The birds were singing softly in the trees, and bees buzzed happily from flower to flower. A mist had formed before sunrise, but was clearing now, leaving wisps across the lake. All was peaceful and quiet in the park.

Tucked away, deep in a hedgerow, underneath leaves and earth, lay Harris and his family in their little house. They had been awake all night, busy searching for food. But now they slept soundly, snoring softly, snuggled up in their beds, warm and comfortable.

Harris twitched his black, shiny nose and sighed contentedly. Not too far away, lay his mother, father and sister Harriet.

Even though they were asleep, they could still hear the faint buzzing of the bees, and the cheerful singing of the birds. It was a nice sound, the sound of a late summer morning bursting into life.

Suddenly, Harris heard something else. Something that made his nose twitch even more, and he opened one eye slowly.

"What was that?" he thought to himself. Maybe he was dreaming. But then the sound became louder. Both eyes snapped open sharply, and he raised his head in annoyance.

"What was that noise? And how dare it wake him from his sleep?" He grunted unhappily and decided to take a look. Stretching quietly so as not to wake the rest of the family, he slipped out of bed, and went to investigate.

The leaves crunched gently beneath his little brown feet, but his parents and sister did not stir.

He blinked wearily, his eyes slowly becoming used to the sunlight. For some moments he could see nothing at all. He looked left and right, and left again.

Nothing.

"Hmm," he said to himself. "I was sure I heard something."

Just as he was about to return to the comfort of his bed, there was the noise again. He turned his head, and sure enough...there they were.

It was a bunch of noisy humans.

There seemed to be quite a lot of them, some big and some small. They were all dressed rather strangely, and they laughed loudly.

Just then, Harris's dad appeared at his side, rubbing his eyes. "Hmm, humans again," he muttered under his breath.

"What are they doing, dad? Don't they know we are trying to sleep?" Harris asked.

"They don't care," his Dad replied, popping a worm into his mouth. "All they're bothered about is meeting up every now and again and running around the park."

Harris looked at the humans angrily; they had woken him, and he was far from happy.

"Why do they do that?" he asked after some thought.

"I don't know. But they do. Rain or shine. They line up, and off they go. Noisy lot. Never think about whether they are disturbing us hedgehogs." His dad grunted and stood with his son watching them.

"How very strange," said Harris.

"Indeed," said his dad. "Humans are very strange things. Don't let it bother you son; come back to bed now, you need your sleep. Lots of foraging to do tonight."

"Just coming," called Harris.

His eyes lingered on the growing crowd for a few seconds more before he turned and went back into the darkness of their home. He lay down in his bed.

His mother and little sister were still sound asleep and had not stirred.

Very soon he was asleep too and dreaming of strangely clothed humans running around the park for no apparent reason at all.

Chapter Two

Exactly one week later to the day, the same thing happened again.

The little hedgehog family were just dropping off to sleep when...

"Morning, everyone!" A human shouted loudly, with absolutely no consideration for any wildlife.

"Oh, for goodness sake!" said Father Hedgehog, which then woke the rest of the family.

Having not long dropped off into a very peaceful doze, and hoping not to be interrupted, they were all very much annoyed, and extremely tired.

"What's going on?" mumbled Mother Hedgehog, her eyes only half open.

"Humans," muttered Father. "Loads of them, all talking far too loudly and jumping around. They get too excited about running around that lake. A lot of commotion about nothing, if you ask me."

"Do you think we should move our house to somewhere a little quieter?" asked Mother.

"No," Father said firmly. "This is our home, and this is where we stay. No human in strange clothing jumping around like an excitable frog is going to force me and my family out of our house!"

Harriet, who was Harris's much younger sister, simply moaned, turned over and went back to sleep. She really couldn't understand what all the fuss was about.

Before his parents could do anything to stop him, Harris had taken matters into his own paws, and had left the safety of their house. He strode across the grass in the direction of the growing crowd.

He stood on his hind legs, at the side of the path, his arms were folded and an angry expression on his face. He was about to give them all a piece of his mind when he stopped and thought for a moment.

Goodness me, weren't they big, close up? Like giants! "I say!" he said, his voice shaking slightly.

No one took any notice whatsoever. He cleared his throat nervously and tried again.

"I say!" he repeated, only this time, a little louder.

Still they took no notice of him but talked between themselves in very loud voices.

Suddenly, one of the humans, a lady, stopped talking and looked at him. Her face loomed down into his, and it startled Harris. He felt very nervous but stood his ground.

"Oh look!" she squealed in delight. "It's a porcupine! Has it escaped from some sort of zoo?"

"It's not a porcupine Margaret, it's a hedgehog," said another human, who had a much gruffer voice.

"Oh. How sweet!" she added, peering at him through very thick spectacles. Her eyes looked huge, like a frog's.

"Wait a minute," added the human called Margaret. "Don't they carry lots of fleas?" She said the last word in a whisper, as though she was embarrassed to even utter it.

Harris was most offended. How very rude of her. Still, he did not move, but he was afraid. One swipe and he would be in their grasp. His only saving grace were his trusty spines.

"Do you think he bites?" wondered Margaret and held out a very bony finger in the direction of his face. It looked huge and ugly, and the fingernail was a bright red colour.

Harris shook from head to toe, and closed his eyes, fearing the worst.

"I wouldn't if I were you," said a voice from behind her.

Harris opened his eyes just enough to see a man with a kind face step in front of the human called Margaret, and politely usher her away. He said some things to her that Harris did not hear.

The man with the nice face bent down on one knee.

"Listen little fellow," he whispered, so as not to frighten the hedgehog. "We will be gone shortly. You can go back to your house and enjoy the rest of your sleep. We will not bother you again today." He smiled in a kind sort of way, stood up and walked away.

"Well, thank you...I..." replied Harris, but the man was gone, disappearing into the mass of the crowd.

Father was waiting for him in the doorway when he returned and seemed very displeased.

"That, young hog, was a very risky move," he said scowling, his arms folded in front of his broad furry chest. "Do you no good you know, talking to humans. I've already told you that they are the ones that drive fast, dangerous things called cars. Although we don't mention that sort of thing in front of your sister." His father sat down in an easy chair made from hollowed-out wood, reached over, pulled out one of his loose spines and picked his teeth with it.

"Dad! So gross when you do that." Harris rolled his eyes.

"Hmm. Gets the grubs out from between my teeth," he explained.

Harris turned away from his dad then and looked out in the direction of the path. The humans had all gone now, and he wondered whether they were all really as bad as his dad said they were.

Chapter Three

A few nights later, the whole family set out to look for food. Darkness had fallen, and the lights from the City were twinkling in the distance.

Their old friend Owl confirmed to them that it was safe to come out and hunt for food. He sat up in his tree, his white feathers gleaming against the night sky. The moon shone behind him, giving the lake a silver glow.

Not many humans were out at this time of night, but there were always a few here and there.

Harris had strayed a little way from the rest of the family, having seen a particularly juicy wood louse up ahead, at the base of a tree. He was very hungry. Licking his lips, he ran after it on all four paws. But the leaves and twigs caught under his tummy and slowed him down. The wood louse got away, disappearing into the roots of the tree.

Moments later, another one appeared, and without thinking, he stood up on his hind legs, very much like he had done that day when he took on the humans. The wood louse was fast, scurrying around up ahead of him through the undergrowth.

Suddenly, he started to run after it, the louse running faster and faster in front of him. He quickened his pace and sure enough, caught up with the speedy grub. With one pounce he was on it! Seconds later he was enjoying a tasty snack and already looking for another.

"That's some impressive running I see," a voice behind him uttered quietly.

Harris gasped and turned around. There, in the light of the lamp post stood the man who had spoken kindly to him only a few days before.

Harris froze.

The man could see that the little hedgehog had been taken completely by surprise. He smiled and bent down again on one knee a few feet away from him.

"Don't be afraid. I'm not going to harm you," he said softly.

Harris was not sure what to do. Dad had always said never to trust a human.

For a few moments they just looked at each other.

"Do you have a name?" asked the man.

"Harris," said Harris, quietly. "Do you?"

"David," said the man. "Very nice to meet you."

"What are you doing in the park after dark?" asked the hedgehog.

"Running. I run here two or three nights a week, as well as Saturday morning."

Harris thought for a moment. "Why?" he asked.

The man smiled. He had grown tired of bending down on one knee and instead had taken a seat on a nearby bench.

"Because I like to. Besides, it's peaceful, and quiet and there's not many people around."

Harris moved a little closer, but not too close. He didn't know this man called David at all, really.

"Why do you all meet up in the morning, once a week? Disturbs our sleep," said Harris. He sat down on the path, a few feet away from the man called David who still sat on the bench.

"It's called a park run," David replied leaning forward. The light from the lamp shone from behind him, making the stripes on his t-shirt glow brightly. "You should come with us one time. You're a pretty good runner yourself."

"Ah, no. It's not for me," Harris said, waving his paw, dismissing the idea. "I only had to try and catch up with that grub just now, because I was so hungry."

"Well," said David, "think about it. Everyone's welcome."

"Thanks." With that, Harris stood up and dusted himself down.

"See you Saturday, then," said David. "And I promise we won't be quite so noisy this time." He smiled, stood up and waved goodbye.

Harris waved back and watched as his new friend
ran off into the darkness.

Chapter Four

After David had gone, Harris realised he was still hungry. He was busy looking for food but also thinking about what David had said.

Over by the lakeside were the juiciest grubs, worms, snails and slugs, but it was a little way further than he normally searched.

He thought for a moment. "I could run there and back. If I get a move on, I won't be gone that long."

He looked behind him to see the rest of the family with their snouts to the ground, looking for something to eat.

"Won't be long!" he shouted over. "Just going a little way up here to see what I can find!"

His mother looked up. "All right then, young man," she called back, "but I want you home in half an hour."

Harris nodded. "Ok Mum!"

He felt a sudden sense of freedom and adventure, so he stood up on his hind legs, and started to run.

At first, he set off too fast and got very out of breath, so he slowed down a little. The night breeze whistled through his spines, and he could feel his heart pounding in his chest.

"This was fun!" he thought to himself. He was now a teenager and relished the spirit of adventure.

Arriving shortly at the lakeside, he stopped and caught his breath. In the undergrowth there was plenty to eat. Snails, slugs, more wood lice and lots of worms. He also found an apple that a human had carelessly thrown away, so he tucked it under his arm with the intention of taking it home to share with the rest of the family.

Once he had eaten, he took a slow, relaxing run back to their house. The night air was cool, with a slight breeze, and Owl hooted, flying from tree to tree, guiding Harris on his way back home. "How lovely it was to be able to run anywhere and everywhere," he thought.

Back at home, Mother thanked him for the apple and straight away Harriet had tucked into it, enjoying the sweet pulp and crisp skin. Juice dripped down her chin, and Father frowned. "Remember your manners, Harriet," he scowled. "At least use a napkin."

"I'm all right Dad," she mumbled with her mouth full.

"When you've finished, it's soon time for bed. Sun

will be up in no time," her father replied. "But you, my lad," he turned to his only son, "I need to have a bit of a man-to-man chat with you."

Harris looked over at his mother. She gave the young hog a knowing look, and then went over to her yoga mat. Assuming the lotus position, she opened one eye which was fixed on her son. She nodded and closed it. A woman of few words was his mum, but he and his sister both knew when it was time to hush and listen.

Once his little sister was in bed and sleeping peacefully, and Mother was well into her tree pose, Harris and his dad sat by the fire together. Now, it has to be said that Harris's father was a very kind hedgehog. His manner was quite abrupt, but he meant well, and had the welfare of his little family at heart. He sat now, in the comfort of his armchair made out of wood, a glass of worm juice swaying gently in his left paw.

The light from the open fire warmed the brown fur on his face, and the reflection of the flames danced in his eyes. Harris watched him in awe. He always looked up to his dad.

Taking a sip of his juice, and heaving a big sigh, the elder hedgehog stared into the flames, and reflected on many things past.

He reached down and playfully poked his only son on the nose, chuckling softly. "Saw you talking to that human this evening, my boy," he said after a while.

Harris did not reply. Instead, he let his father do the

talking. There would be plenty of time to give his side of the story.

"He seems a decent sort, I suppose. But all the same, one of those that likes galloping around the lake for no reason." He took another sip of his drink.

From over the other side of the room out of the gloom came his mother's voice. She was now doing a shoulder stand, but still managed to speak.

"Tell him the story, Spike."

His dad gave a deep sigh.

"Like running, do you?"

"Yes Dad, I think I do," replied the young hedgehog.

"Well, that's jolly good. Back in my day, when I was a lad, not much older than you, I liked to have a bit of a run myself."

Harris gasped. "Did you really?" he whispered.

"It was a very, very long time ago. I was a young hog. Full of spirit, just like you," Spike tapped his nose and winked.

Harris almost held his breath, waiting for the next instalment of the story.

"So? What happened, Dad?"

"Well," his father replied after a short pause, "I got really into my running. Ran everywhere, all of the time. Loved it. Not with humans though, it has to be said, just on my own. Then one day, I was hurtling along at top speed, so fast down this hill, where we used to live, and disaster struck."

"Oh no!" cried Harris, and he put his paw to his mouth.

"Yes indeed," continued his dad. "I was running so fast that I fell over and went into a roll, all the way down the hill and straight into a tree. Knocked myself out, I did."

"This was becoming a very exciting story," thought the little hedgehog. He urged his father to carry on to the end.

"When I woke up, I was back in the burrow I shared with my parents, and my two brothers, your Uncle Prickles and your Uncle Knuckles. Hmmm. Had a bit of a headache I did, and every spine on my back had a leaf stuck to it, very annoying. Took your grandmother 3 days to get rid of them. She said I looked like somebody's hedge."

"Goodness me, Dad, that's awful. Did it put you off running for good?"

"It did for a while. Didn't run for a few years after that, and then I met your mother, and my priorities in life changed. I sort of forgot about running really, until I saw you tonight. Brought a lot of old memories flooding back."

"Good ones as well as bad ones," added Harris quietly.

"Well, what I'm trying to say is, it taught me two things, which I will now pass on to you. Don't ever run too fast that your little legs can't cope with the speed, and..." he whispered closer to his son, "your mother and I think you need a decent pair of trainers, like that human, David."

Harris gasped. "Could I really have a pair like that?"

"If you're serious about going running with the park run lot, then you need something sturdy. We'll get you a pair before they come again."

The little hedgehog could not believe his ears.

"Thanks Dad! Thanks Mum!" he said excitedly.

"Off to bed now young man," his mother replied firmly. "You've got to get your rest."

With that, the little hog obediently did as he was told, and was soon dreaming of a very nice pair of brand new running shoes.

Chapter Five

The following day, after Mother had finished the children's lessons, she gathered up her bag, made from the leaf of a rhubarb plant, placed three large worms in it and a big fat juicy blackberry. The fruit had been early that year, largely due, Spike had said, to having plenty of rain over the summer months.

"Come along you two," she ordered. "Time to go and see Mr. Montgomery Mouse to get Harris some running shoes."

Now, Mr Montgomery Mouse, or "Mont the Meesh" as he was commonly known, had a small shop not far away, which was attached to his house. He sold pretty much everything, and could turn his hand to most things, which included, on the odd occasion, shoes.

As you can imagine, shoes were not commonly worn by the folk who lived in the woods, but every now and again, the need did arise.

Mother opened the door to the little shop, and the bell rang to let the occupants know they had customers.

Harris and his sister loved it here. Mont the Meesh's wife was very fond of baking apple pies out the back, and the smell of freshly cooked apple, the heady aroma of cinnamon and fresh buttery pastry filled the little shop to the brim. They raised their snouts to catch the delicious smells coming from the kitchen.

From behind the curtain which led 'out back' appeared Mont the Meesh. He was a small grey mouse, not very tall, with a wide middle. Mother said it was because he ate too many of his wife's apple pies. "Good afternoon, Mr Montgomery," Mother said proudly, setting down her bag.

"Good afternoon, Mrs Hedgehog, and what can I do for you today?" he replied politely, showing four alarmingly large teeth.

"I'd like a wide-toothed comb please, for Harriet's spines, they're getting a little unruly the older she gets... a nightmare to keep a ribbon in. Oh, and I wonder if you wouldn't mind measuring up Harris here, for some running shoes?"

Mont the Meesh raised his eyebrows and rubbed his chin thoughtfully.

"Running shoes? he repeated slowly. "Hmm." He went over to a shelf on the far side of the shop to get the comb Mother had requested and put it down on the counter.

"That'll be one large blackberry, please Mrs H," he said firmly.

Mother reached down and rummaged around in her bag. She took out the blackberry and set it down on the counter.

"Ah! Fine looking specimen!" he exclaimed with delight. "Now then, shoes, shoes, shoes," he looked deep in thought for a moment.

After a while of walking around the shop looking for something, he finally found his tape measure in a drawer, which he unravelled and placed neatly around his neck.

"Just need to measure the young man's feet first, Mrs H."

"Yes, of course," said Mother, and motioned her son to go and sit on a chair over on the other side of the room.

Mont the Meesh strode over and took the tape from around his neck. He bent over, revealing a little bit too much bottom out of the seat of his trousers.

Harriet giggled, but soon stopped when Mother threw her a stern look. She looked away and decided to try out her new comb instead.

"Small feet," said Mont after some moments of measuring. He looked over the top of his glasses.

Harris the Hedgehog
And His Running Adventure

First published in 2018

Copyright © AV Turner 2018

The rights of the author and illustrator have been asserted in accordance with Sections 77 and 78 of the Copyright Designs and Patents Act, 1988.

ISBN-13: 978-1720617877

Follow: @AVTurnerAuthor

TEAMAUTHOR UK

Publishing with you

To my late mother, Janet

And all young runners...everywhere.

"But, I think I might have something out back that will do very well indeed. Just give me a second."

Mother smiled in agreement.

Harriet ran over to her brother and whispered something in his ear; they both giggled.

"Children!" scolded Mother in a hushed voice. "Enough!" She knew exactly what they were giggling about, and it most certainly involved Mr Montgomery Mouse and his tightly fitting trousers.

Shortly, Mont the Meesh reappeared from behind his curtain carrying a pale brown box.

"Now then," he said proudly, "last year I made these for another client of mine, a certain Franklyn Ferret. Very fast on his feet, he was. But unfortunately, he never got to wear them. They have stayed in the box ever since. Brand new, never been worn, such a shame."

"Oh dear," said Mother. "Did the poor chap meet with some sort of accident?"

"No," replied Mont the Meesh abruptly. "Took up tap dancing instead."

"Oh," said Mother.

"Anyway, if my measurements are correct, these beauties should fit our young man here very nicely."

He opened the box with care, and there inside were the most wonderful pair of running shoes Harris had ever seen. He gasped in amazement. They were bright red, with black laces.

Mother clapped her hands in delight. Harris tried them on quickly and tied up the laces carefully. He ran up and down the little shop, and then jumped up and down on the spot.

"Do they fit?" asked Mont the Meesh.

"They're perfect!" confirmed Harris. "I love them!"

"I can't thank you enough Mr Montgomery," beamed Mother. "How much for those?"

Mont the Meesh made a sucking noise with his teeth. "A little more expensive, Mrs H. Specialised item, you see," he rubbed his chin with his paw again. "But for you, I'll say 4 worms and an apple. Medium-sized."

"I only have three worms in my bag, but I can acquire another, plus the apple to secure the payment," said Mother.

"Not a problem Mrs H," replied Mont the Meesh. "Being as it's you. You and your husband are very good customers of mine, I'll put it on your tab. Anytime within the next few days will be fine. You can take the shoes with you today."

"Why, thank you so very much Mr Montgomery,"
Mother said and held out her paw, which he
shook heartily.

"Pleasure doing business with you," he replied.

With that, the children and their mother left the
shop. Harriet and her mother walked, but Harris,
keen to try out his new running shoes, ran all the
way home.

Chapter Six

Later that evening, Harris had still not taken his shoes off, but was admiring them whilst he sat with his father in front of the fire.

"Very fine pair of running shoes," said Spike. "Worth that little bit extra I think, my lovely," he commented over his shoulder to his wife. She nodded in agreement and went once again over to her yoga mat, assuming her usual lotus position.

Harris's eyes gleamed with excitement. He couldn't wait to try them out.

"I'm going to take the lad out for a while," added Spike. "Give these bad boys a test run. Won't be long."

His mother simply nodded and closed her eyes. "Don't go wearing them out," she added.

Outside, the night was cooler than usual. Harris and his dad could see their breath in the air.

All was still. There was no one around, only the wise old owl, up in the tree, keeping watch.

Spike went and sat over on a log at the side of the path. He crossed his legs, took out a little flask filled with worm juice, and unscrewed the top slowly.

"Now then, my lad," he said thoughtfully after taking a sip of it, burping quietly and then excusing himself. "A few basic things you need to know about running before you start doing it seriously."

"I don't need leg warmers?" Harris quickly replied.

"Erm, no. You don't need leg warmers, Son. What are they anyway?" His dad looked confused.

"Like socks but without feet in them. I don't want to wear those, they look really silly."

"No, no, no," said Spike. "All you need are a good pair of shoes and some passion for the sport. That's all."

He shifted around to get comfortable on the log, cleared his throat and carried on with the training speech.

"Now then. The first thing is, don't set off too quick. You'll get out of breath. Just remember, you've got some ground to cover, so just go steady and run the mile you're in."

"But, I get so excited Dad, I want to go fast!"

Spike put up his paw. "No Son, you will get out of breath, and your body will run out of energy way before you get to where you want to be. You need to pace yourself."

Harris took a deep sigh. He was getting a little bit bored of Dad lecturing him about stuff. He just wanted to be off and running.

"If you don't listen, you will get injured, my boy, and then you won't be able to run at all for a while."

"Okaaaay," the young hog replied, rolling his eyes.

He stood in the middle of the path with his hands on his hips, kicking the stones.

"Don't do that, you'll ruin those shoes and they're brand new. We paid good worms for those. Now then," continued his dad, taking another swig of the juice and wiping his mouth with the back of his paw. "If you do get a bit tired, slow up a little, give your body time to recover, then when you feel stronger, go a bit faster."

Suddenly, out of the darkness, they heard a sound. Spike hopped off his log and motioned Harris to come off the path and into the undergrowth. They could hear someone breathing heavily, and the sound of footsteps quickly coming towards them.

"It's David!" cried Harris, and he held up his paw as his friend ran into the lamplight.

"Goodness me!" cried the runner. "Good evening you two, off out foraging again?" He stood for a moment out of breath.

"Hi David," replied Harris. "Erm, this is my dad; he's giving me some running lessons, look at my new shoes!"

David crouched down and studied the young hog's shiny new footwear and nodded.

"Very impressive!" he said. "Bet they cost a bit."

"Money in fair words," replied Spike, haughtily.

Harris looked at his dad. "Be nice. He's OK, as humans go."

"Worth it if he's going to take it seriously...erm, David is it?"

"Yes, how do you do? Nice to meet you…"

"Spike's the name."

"Ah yes, Spike. Very pleased to meet you."

The two of them shook hands and David took a moment to sit down on the park bench again and chat.

For about half an hour they discussed the basic rules of running, and Spike found David to be a very agreeable sort of chap. He even offered him some worm juice, but David declined politely.

Harris felt he had learnt quite a lot from both of them, and eventually David stood up. "Listen, I've got to go now, because my wife and children will be at home waiting for me as well, but please come along to the park run on Saturday? Anyone can join in. Try and get some practice runs in before then if you can."

Harris looked at his dad. "Can I?"

"Of course! But, like David says, you need some practice first."

"Ok then, David," Harris replied. "I'll see you there!"

"Great," said David and once again he disappeared off into the darkness, his footsteps echoing into the night.

After one lap of the lake, and a few runs up and down some little hills, Harris and his dad headed for home, very tired indeed. They didn't forget however, to stop off and collect a few worms and grubs, as Harriet and Mother would surely be hungry.

Chapter Seven

The next few nights saw the pair out regularly on training sessions. When it was nearly midnight, Mother and Harriet would forage for food, and the two males would disappear off to the lakeside.

Sometimes, Spike would run alongside his son, but got out of breath really quickly.

"Phew!" his dad let out a big sigh. "Need to lose a few pounds," Spike exclaimed patting his ample tummy. "Trouble is, I've got a thing for slugs. Your mother always says, 'a moment on the lips, a lifetime on the hips'; I think she's right, my lad."

"Slugs are your favourite though, Dad," agreed the young hog.

"It's only if they're in the house, under my nose, you see. Can't leave them alone." Spike shook his head.

Harris smiled. He was thinking about the race with David and the other humans, which was only two days away. He felt a little nervous, but excited at the same time.

Spike stopped rubbing his ample tummy and walked over to his son.

"Know what you need?" he said thoughtfully.

Harris shook his head.

"A little bit of cross training, goes a long way to strengthen those muscles. Come with me!"

Spike put his arm around his son's shoulders, and the two of them walked briskly in the direction of Mr Montgomery Mouse's shop.

It's true to say that this store never closed. It was open 24 hours a day, and well known throughout the park that Mrs Mouse's apple pies were always equally available. She was permanently up to her elbows in pastry and flour, with apples cooking gently on the stove, smothered in cinnamon and sugar.

The two hedgehogs could smell the sweetness of the fruit cooking as they opened the door, and the bell announced their arrival.

Through the curtain from 'out back' came Mont the Meesh, wiping his paws on a small towel.

"Mr Spike!" he exclaimed, smiling broadly. "What a pleasure it is sir, to see you, and young Harris here." The little mouse raised both arms up in the air and then clapped his paws in delight. "Now, what can I do for you this evening? I trust the running shoes are to your satisfaction?" Mont looked a little concerned and rubbed his chin.

"Perfect! Couldn't be better, thank you so much, Mr Montgomery." Spike put his arm on the counter and leant over as if to speak to the mouse in confidence. He looked around the shop so as no one could hear, but as there was no one else, it seemed pretty unnecessary to Harris.

"The truth is," whispered Spike, "the boy is doing a race, two days from now. Wants to do well, but those little legs need building up a bit, you know. I've told him he needs to cross train."

Mont the Meesh also leaned over from the other side of the counter. "I see." He rubbed his chin again and the two of them turned and looked at the young hog.

"What?" Harris asked awkwardly.

"I've got just the thing, out back, Mr Spike. Bear with me, won't you?" With that, Mr Montgomery Mouse disappeared through the curtain.

Moments later, he reappeared pushing something that squeaked loudly. Harris could not see as the counter, and a large sack of grain, masked his view, but very soon all became clear.

"By jove," exclaimed Spike. "What a marvellous specimen! You have surpassed yourself this time, my friend!" He clapped his paws in delight and rubbed them together with glee.

"Now then, my boy," said Mont the Meesh. "This will help build those muscles up in your young legs! Cross training is rather important for runners, like yourself."

He proudly presented a small, black, three-wheeled trike, a little rusty in places, and carrying a rather loud squeak. Two of the tyres were flat, and there was a basket on the back of it.

The three of them looked at it in silence. Harris's heart sank.

Mont the Meesh sensed that Harris was not really that impressed. "Needs a little tweaking, here and there. But give me a few minutes and I can have it ready for you. A little oil, and I'll pump up the tyres." He shuffled his feet nervously and darted a quick look over to Spike. "You can borrow it, if you like for a few days until you do your race."

"Thank you very much Mr Montgomery," said Harris's dad as the chain fell off, and the final tyre went flat, sounding for all the world like a squashed whoopy cushion.

Chapter Eight

True to his word, as he always was, of course, Mont the Meesh did indeed have the little trike up and running within a short space of time. The tyres were plumped up, the squeak was replaced by perfect silence, and the chain was fixed. A quick rub down with some wood louse ear wax, and it was good to go.

Harris was suitably impressed with the transformation, and hopped on, eager to give it a try. He flicked the bell with his paw and beamed with delight.

"Thank you, Mr Montgomery Mouse," he said, looking over his shoulder, and with that, was off down the track, away from the shop.

Spike had given the shopkeeper a gift of two fat slugs and an apple as a way of saying thank you. He also knew that this meant more apple pies would come from Mrs Mouse's kitchen.

Harris rode the little bike for hours, up and down the tracks in the park, going so fast at times that leaves and dust would fly out from under the back wheels as he sped away.

Spike stood proudly and watched his son. His determination alone would see him through on the day of the run. The little hedgehog was unrelenting when it came to training.

After two laps of the lake, he screeched to a halt in front of his dad.

"Rest time now, my boy," ordered the elder. "Getting enough rest is equally as important as training hard. Remember that." He patted Harris on the shoulder and they both returned home, putting the bike safely in the little shed at the side of the house just in case it rained. A rusty bike would be of no use at all, and it was always a good idea to take care of things, especially when someone was kind enough to trust you with their property.

Before bed, his mother had suggested he join her on the yoga mat for a few stretches. Afterwards, he felt much better and slept very well indeed.

The following day, just before dusk, and on the eve of the run, Harris was about to put on his running shoes, when his mum stopped him.

"Not tonight, my love," she shook her head but smiled kindly. "Save up your energy for tomorrow morning. You'll need it!"

"But I want to go out and train, Mum," the young hog protested.

"No," she said firmly. "Tonight, you rest; come and forage with us by all means, but no bike ride, and no running. Big day tomorrow and I want you to get some sleep tonight, even if it's just a few hours. You can't run the race when you are tired, Harris."

He knew not to argue with his mother and did as he was told. He busied himself gathering food for the family, and even found a very large juicy apple, which he decided to save and give to Mr Montgomery Mouse by way of a thank you for all he had done for him. It was the least he could do.

By midnight, he was safely tucked up in bed. His parents and sister kissed him goodnight, and placed his newly cleaned running shoes close by, ready for the following morning.

"Big day tomorrow, Son," whispered his dad.

Chapter Nine

The morning of the race dawned. Birds sang happily in the trees and chatted together excitedly. The sun shone brightly overhead, and flowers turned their faces towards it, smiling and welcoming the warmth it brought them.

Over at the shop, Mr Montgomery Mouse and his wife had finished their breakfast and were busy washing their whiskers. Once they had both put on their hats and Mrs Mouse had applied a little lipstick, they closed up the shop and set off to watch the race. Mrs Mouse wanted to watch Harris set off, and Mr Mouse wanted to watch him finish, so in order to do both successfully, they had decided to use the trike.

The home of the Hedgehogs was a hive of activity. Spike was preparing breakfast, Harriet was trying desperately to get her new comb through her spines and help Mother with a banner they had prepared to cheer Harris on. Time was running out, and Harris was getting very nervous. He put on his running shoes and did a few stretches.

"Time to go, everyone," shouted his dad, and with that they all hurried out of the house.

Over by the pathway, a crowd had started to gather. Harris could see his friend David, and the human called Margaret. A number of his woodland friends had come to cheer him on too and stood under a tree nearby waving little flags.

"Good morning, Harris!" David bent down and shook his little friend's paw. "Good luck today!"

"Thank you. Good luck to you too!" Harris gulped nervously.

"Don't worry, you will be just great. Relax and enjoy it. Remember what your dad told you...don't set off too quick, or you'll run out of energy."

"Ok. Thanks," Harris replied.

A human in ordinary clothes stood over on the other side of the path and gave everyone instructions about staying safe on the run. Apparently, there would be people along the route who would help you know where to go.

Harris took his place amongst the others at the start line and breathed deeply. Next to him was David and lining the side of the path were his family. Mother and Harriet were holding a banner high up in the air which read 'Run Harris, Run!' Harriet squealed with delight and excitement and jumped up and down. Spike stood nervously with his arms folded across his chest, and to Harris's delight he saw some late arrivals, his Uncle Knuckles and Uncle Prickles had come to watch too!! He had not seen them since Christmas. They were both very busy hogs working as security guards at a dance hall right on the edge of the park.

Harris gave everyone a little wave and waited. Suddenly he heard a whistle and the race began!

He remembered what his dad and David had said to him and he started off quite slowly.

"Good luck brother!" shouted Harriet. "I'm so proud of you!"

Harris beamed with pride.

Once his family and friends were out of view, he was able to concentrate on the race. Some of the humans had passed him and were way up front. David however, stayed alongside his new running buddy and shouted words of encouragement.

"Don't worry about what they're doing. Just focus on your own race. I'll stay with you for your first one, make sure you're OK."

"Thanks!" puffed Harris and they ran on.

The route took them two laps of the lake, then over the little wooden bridge, through the Japanese garden, and the finish line was over the far side of the park, very close to where the ice cream van stood.

Harris liked the thought of ice cream, but he knew that milk and dairy was bad for hedgehogs and made them poorly. Still, no harm in dreaming about it.

They were almost at the end of their first lap of the lake, when Harris started to feel a little bit tired. David had noticed he had dropped back slightly, so he also altered his pace accordingly.

"Slow it right down, if you're struggling," he whispered. "It doesn't matter how long it takes you, just concentrate on getting over the finish line."

Harris nodded. He knew he had to be careful and save some energy for the rest of the race.

They ran on into their second lap of the lake when all of a sudden something caught his eye. There, trundling alongside them, was a sight to be behold.

Mrs Mouse was pedalling industriously on the little trike that he had borrowed only days before but attached to the back of it was an old dolls' pram, bumping along merrily. In the pram were Mr Mouse, and the rest of the hedgehog family.

Harris's mother and father were desperately trying to hold on and wave the banner at the same time while Uncles Knuckles and Prickles steered it as best they could to stop it tipping over.

"Go on, lad!" shouted Spike. "You can do it!" and he waved frantically at his son as Mrs Mouse pedalled faster to keep up with the crowd of runners.

This spurred the young hog on even more. He beamed at his family and looked up towards David. Seeing them cheering him on gave Harris the determination he needed.

Very soon, they were nearing the second lap of the lake and almost half way there.

It was now that Harris felt his most comfortable. His muscles were nicely warmed up, and he could feel power and strength surging through his body. David looked down from time to time, and gave a thumbs-up, which he guessed meant that all was going well.

Turning a sharp corner, they then ran through the Japanese gardens, which were very pretty indeed during the daytime. Even with Autumn fast approaching, the flowers and plants still held their colour.

Harris guessed that they could be near the end, but he still felt good. His spines tingled and the air was pleasantly warm. Running made him feel so wonderful, that he had already decided that this was what he wanted to do every week with his new friends.

"Just a little way further, Harris and we are at the finish line!" said David. He was quite out of breath now, but the wind whistled through his hair, and he looked so happy.

David pointed to something in the distance. "There it is!"

With that, the little hedgehog made an extra effort, and with the end in sight, ran faster than he had ever done in his life.

He could just see everyone waiting for him, and cheering.

With an extra spurt of energy, he and David crossed over the finish line! What a wonderful feeling it was! He felt proud, not only of himself but of everyone who had ran the race.

"Fantastic effort," cried David.

"Thank you very much!" he beamed and ran over to his family and friends who were waiting to congratulate him.

When Mother and the rest of the clan had hugged him excitedly, Harris made his way over to David who was sitting on a bench eating a banana.

"Well done, my friend. Did you enjoy that?"

"I certainly did," replied Harris grinning from ear to ear.

They shook hands and Harris sighed contentedly. Looking down at his running shoes, he felt very happy with himself indeed.

David reached into his backpack and took something bright and gleaming out of it. Finishing his banana and placing the yellow skin in the waste bin next to him, he was able to take the mystery object in both hands.

"This is for you," he smiled.

"Why, thank you," whispered Harris. "What is it?"

"A medal," replied David and he placed the red ribbon around the little hog's neck. A bright shiny disc nestled against his chest.

"My little girl made it for you," added David. "You are quite the most remarkable little hedgehog I have ever met, and I am very proud to call you my running partner."

Harris felt that he could not be happier and grinned from ear to ear.

"Same time next week then?" asked David.

"Absolutely," replied the little hog.

Chapter Ten

After the excitement of the day had calmed down, and the family were all back at home, Harris sat in front of the fire with Spike and admired his medal.

It was true to say that Father was more than proud of his son.

"Are you going to carry on running now then, my boy?"

"Oh yes Dad," he replied quietly, "most definitely."

"Pardon the pun, but I think you just may have 'the running bug'," chuckled Spike, taking a large gulp of worm juice.

Harris smiled to himself.

"Night, Dad. I'm going to turn in now, really tired."

He left his father snoring softly in the chair, kissed his mother goodnight and was very happy to get into bed.

Harris lay on his side, clutching the medal in both paws, stroking it.

Very soon he fell asleep and dreamed of running races. But not just small ones, big races all over the world, far beyond the park gates.

He did not realise it yet, but running had not only given him happiness, strength and determination, it had also blessed him with a new-found confidence.

He was capable of doing whatever he put his mind to.

It just goes to prove, that even the smallest of creatures can make a big impact on the world.

THE END

Acknowledgements

As always, gratitude and love to my wonderful dad, Harry who is permanently by my side throughout the whole writing process.

Thanks to my mum, who although no longer with us, still guides and nurtures her youngest child in all things artistic.

To Sue Miller, my hardworking Editor, who never fails to impress me with her dedication and passion.

Thanks to my beautiful daughter Freya, for not only proof-reading this book many times, but also doing me the honour of a lovely illustration, and being quite the best daughter in the universe. To my husband Richard for checking over the text and giving an approving nod.

Much gratitude to my great friend Kara, for the most beautiful illustrations that I could have wished for. Thank you for your loyalty, friendship and hard work. We had so much fun on this project.

Finally, a posthumous thank you to a very dear friend, who will unfortunately never get to see the final publication of this book but will forever be in our hearts. Alastair, your kindness, friendship and unfailing belief in my work will never be forgotten, my friend. We miss you.

About the Author

AV Turner was born and raised in Nottingham. She started writing when she was just a little girl. Her fascination with hedgehogs started at a very early age, and she now owns her very own pet hog, Harris. A keen runner, she lives in rural Shropshire with her family.

Printed in Great Britain
by Amazon